The Night They Nicked Saint Nick

Carl Ashmore

DEDICATION

For Alice – as everything is.

For Miss Gadsby, Mrs Horton, Mrs Proudman and the other staff of Brierley Primary School, Crewe.

For the pupils of Brierley Primary School - especially Eeshana, Imogen, Eloise, James-Stuart, Ashton, Sophie, Lewis, Amy, Leo J, Darja, Lydia, Rebecca, Jacob, Leah Rose, Jake, Carly, Matthew, Leo W, Aaliyah and Dorothy

CHAPTERS

IN MEMORY OF BERNARD ASHMORE

Chapter 1

Munkle's Arrival

Christmas had come to Crewe, and it made Derek Brundle dizzy with delight and joy.

You see, Derek adored Christmas. He loved fat mince pies and even fatter Christmas puddings. He loved the smell of turkey bubbling in the oven and the shimmering lights, colouring his eyes green and red, on the colossal tree that filled his lounge. He even loved the woolly jumper Granny Brundle knitted him every year, which itched and prickled and was large enough to fit a baby hippopotamus.

Yes, it was safe to say that Derek

loved everything about Christmas.

And most of all, he loved Santa Claus.

Each Christmas Eve, just before bedtime, he would leave the plumpest and juiciest mince pie on his bedside cabinet for Santa to find when he delivered his presents, and would always hand-pick not one, but a clump of chubby carrots to make sure all the reindeers had something tasty to eat for their long night ahead.

And so it was, on this particular Christmas Eve, that Derek woke with a start from a lifelike dream – a dream in which he'd been kidnapped, taken to a dark, scary Scottish castle and locked in a cold and musty dungeon.

But it wasn't the dream that caused his head to spin like a top. It was the fact that staring into his dressing table mirror, he could see a thick tuft of wiry grey hair, just above his right ear. *Grey hair?* Being only seven, he had no wish to turn grey until he'd reached his Uncle Bertrum's age, at the very least. Before he had time to panic, however, he heard a strange sound.

TAP TAP.

It came from the window.

Derek's stomach did a little flip. His first thought was that a branch from a nearby tree had rapped the glass, but then he remembered there were no trees in his back garden. His second thought was that a short-sighted robin had crash landed, but that was an even sillier thought than his first one.

TAP TAP TAP.

There it was again.

He stepped nervously towards the window and flung open the curtains. What he saw made his eyes swell to the size of gobstoppers.

Outside, hovering in mid-air was a tiny, cherry haired woman wearing a black jumpsuit and a red beret with a bobble crafted from gold tinsel. She pointed frantically at the window, pleading with Derek to let her in.

Too stunned to object, Derek opened the window.

'Hello-ho-ho, Derek,' the little woman said chirpily, soaring into his bedroom and landing on the carpet. 'Sorry to barge in like this.' She reached down and pulled off what looked like a pair of flippers. 'Ah, that's better. These *hover-shoes* kill me tootsies.'

Derek stood frozen to the spot. 'Who – who are you?'

'Munkle.' The woman stood rigid and saluted. Even at full height, she barely came up to Derek's waist. 'Captain Elleana Munkle. S.E.S.'

'S - E - S?' Derek spluttered.

'Special Elf Service,' Munkle replied. 'It's an honour to meet you,

Derek.'

'Elf service?'

'Yeppers'

'You're an elf?'

'With the pointy ears to prove it.' Munkle turned her head to reveal a set of very pointy ears.

Derek fell speechless. 'But … I don't understand.'

Munkle took a deep breath. 'Course you don't. And I'm afraid I don't have time to explain. We 'ave to be going.'

'Going?' Derek panted. 'Go where?'

'To Poleland.' Munkle noticed the patch of grey on Derek's head and gave a high-pitched squeak. 'Prancer's Potty!'

'What's the matter?'

Munkle composed herself. 'Tell you later. We have to go now. We're runnin' outta time.' Munkle pulled a larger pair of hover-shoes from her jumpsuit and passed them to Derek. "Ere, put these on.'

'But – but I can't go anywhere.'

'You must,' Munkle replied. 'Without you there'll be no Christmas!'

Derek looked flabbergasted. 'What?'

'No Christmas,' Munkle repeated glumly.

'What do you mean no Christmas?'

Munkle paused for a moment. 'Okey mokey, I'll tell you a bit… Krinkle told me not to, but what does she know? She's only a thousand years old and the wisest elf in Poleland. Anyhow, you'd better sit down or you're likely to get the leggy wobbles and fall down.'

Derek sat promptly on his bed.

Munkle tapped a finger against her chin. 'There's no easy way to say this, so I'll just say it … you're the next Santa Claus.'

Derek's face crumpled. 'I'm the next – '

'Santa Claus, that's right! Now, you're not due to take over for another fourteen years. But, unfortunately, the current one has … erm … gone missing. Therefore, you're needed to deliver presents to six billion manfolk, by tomorrow morning.' Munkle smiled weakly. 'Okey mokey?'

Derek struggled to keep up. 'What do you mean "gone missing"?'

Munkle gave a heavy sigh. 'He's been kidnapped…'

'Kidnapped? By who?'

'We don't know,' Munkle replied miserably. 'We know he's still alive, but that's all. Besides, even if we did know where he was it's probably too late to find the old fella. That's why we need you...'

Derek looked like he'd been hit on the head with a shovel. 'But … I – I can't be Santa Claus.'

'And why not?'

'Because I'm seven.'

'All the Santas were seven once.'

Derek gulped. 'All the Santas?'

'Yeppers. There've been thirteen so far. You see, a new Santa is born every hundred and fifty years, and each one, like you, has no idea it's them. That is, until they turn twenty one, become Santa, and bring joy to manfolk everywhere, as well as keepin' six thousand elves and eight thousand trolls in jobs in Poleland.'

Derek couldn't believe his ears. He was the new Santa Claus? The current Santa had been kidnapped? There were thousands of elves and trolls living in somewhere called Poleland?

'You're gonna faint, aren't you?'

Munkle said, studying Derek closely.

'No,' Derek replied.

'Good,' Munkle said. 'So tell me you'll come. We're all depending on you!'

'But what about my mum and dad?' Derek asked. 'They'll be up in half an hour. They'll expect me to be here.'

'Don't worry 'bout them,' Munkle rooted through her pocket and pulled out what looked like a can of deodorant. 'This is dozy spray. One squirt of this and they'll be fast asleep for as long as is necessary.'

Derek eyed the can suspiciously. 'Is it safe?'

'Course,' Munkle replied. 'So long as they're not allergic to it.'

'And what happens if they are?'

'They grow an extra nose for a couple of days.' Munkle watched as a look of horror crossed Derek's face.

'But I've only known that to happen once and it was with a test troll.'

'A test troll?'

'Yeppers. We have to test new products on summat and Santa insists on no animal testing. Troll's volunteer.' Munkle shrugged. 'They're as stupid as snowflakes.'

'It grew another nose?'

'Yeppers, but don't worry, trolls grow new body parts all the time. I know one with seven ankles.' Munkle smiled. 'So, Derek Brundle, will you help us save Christmas?'

Derek sighed. 'But how can I help? I'm just an ordinary boy.'

Munkle's eyes twinkled. 'You couldn't be more special, Derek. You just don't know it yet.' Then she moved closer and whispered in his ear. 'Come with me. I'll show you things you couldn't imagine in your most fantoobulous dreams...'

And Derek agreed. What choice did he have? The world needed Christmas and if he could help in any way he would. He did, however, wonder what his dad might say if he had to tuck into Christmas dinner with a second nose.

Chapter 2

Flight of the Sprite

According to Munkle, there was no time for Derek to change out of his pyjamas, so whilst she left the room waving the can of dozy spray, Derek slipped into his navy blue dressing gown and slippers.

Munkle returned seconds later. 'Job done.'

'How do we wake them up? Derek asked anxiously.

Munkle produced a second canister. 'This is wakey wakey spray. One squirt of this and they'll wake up in a flash. Now, if you could put on your hover-shoes, we'll be on our way.'

Derek watched Munkle slip into her hover-shoes and followed her lead.

'Right,' Munkle said, checking to see Derek's hover-shoes were securely fixed. 'Follow me.' She leapt through the window and a moment later was floating like a balloon, grinning from ear to ear. Derek followed hesitantly onto the window ledge.

'Nowt to worry about,' Munkle said, and she started to do a little dance as if to prove that everything was safe.

'Are you sure about this?' Derek asked, his back pressed firmly against the window.

'Course.'

'But I'm heavier than you.'

Munkle grinned. 'I've seen the same model hover-shoe lift a teddy bear the size of your house.'

Derek knew it was pointless arguing, so he closed his eyes and stepped out. It was the strangest feeling, as though his foot had landed on a warm cushion. He opened his eyes, looked down and gasped. He hovered more than twenty feet from the ground.

'Told you,' Munkle said, holding out her hand. 'Now, grab my mittsy.'

Derek took her hand and suddenly they were gliding upwards, his tummy rolling and lurching as though in an invisible lift. Even through the heavy fog, he could see the wakening houses spread before him like a twinkling map. 'We're not flying to Poleland, are we?' he said, pulling his dressing gown tight to combat the cold.

Munkle chuckled. 'Not in hover-shoes we're not.'

'Then how are we -' But before

Derek could finish, they had landed on the roof. Derek's eyes widened as he saw what looked like an oversized toy car; painted blue and red, it had silver headlights and no roof. 'We're driving there?' he said with disbelief.

'That would take a week.' Munkle said, taking off her hover-shoes. 'No, this is the Sprite 1200 - the fastest aerocar in the world.'

'It can fly?' Derek said.

'Faster than any manfolk plane,' Munkle replied. 'Hop in.' She opened the driver's door and settled onto the seat. A slightly baffled Derek opened the passenger door and sat down. There was very little room and Derek found his knees curled up against his head.

'Sorry 'bout the squeeze, but the Sprite 1200 is designed for elfkind not manfolk.' Munkle pressed a green button and a clear plastic roof slid over their heads, sealing them in. At the same time, a series of dials and knobs burst into life and the little car shook and shuddered. Then it rose slowly into the air.

'Where is Poleland?' Derek said, desperately trying to forget he was in a flying car. 'The North Pole?'

'The South Pole - there's nowt at the North Pole but ice and water. Actually, the thinkin' that Santa lived at the North Pole was just a rumour Krinkle started years ago, to stop manfolk looking for it.'

'Who's Krinkle?'

'She's chief elf - been High Commissioner for over six hundred years. I'm not sure Christmas'd happen at all if it wasn't for ol' Krinkly.'

'What does she do?' Derek asked.

'She organises everything: work schedules for elves and trolls, delivery plans, production rotas. She even makes sure Santa's suit is washed and pressed for the big day. This Santa's not the most organised we've ever had.' Munkle smiled warmly, then glanced at Derek and her face grew sad. 'Still, he's my favourite one so far.'

When the Sprite 1200 was about fifty foot in the air it came to a halt. Munkle turned to Derek. 'We've eleven thousand three hundred and twelve miles to fly in an hour, so I'll be using the Hyper-thrusters.'

Derek gulped. 'What does that mean?'

'It means you're in for the ride of your life, kidder.' Munkle winked at Derek. 'You up for it?'

Derek didn't have time to reply. A loud *POP* cut the silence and – WHOOOSH - the aerocar rocketed away like a firework, leaving Derek's house far behind.

As far as Derek was concerned, it all became a blur. He didn't have time to be worried or frightened or excited; they were flying at such unbelievable speeds it was like time itself had stopped. They reached a cruising height in a matter of seconds.

Munkle cast Derek a kindly smile. 'That's the worst of it over.'

After the initial shock of take off, the journey could only be described as very smooth indeed. Derek watched eagerly through the window but, as they were travelling so fast, couldn't make out anything clearly. He did, however, have something else on his mind. 'Can I ask you something, Munkle? Why do you sometimes wince when you look at me?'

Munkle began to say something and then stopped herself. When she finally spoke, her words were little more than a whisper. 'I think Santa's fading.'

'Fading?' Derek asked.

Munkle's eyes grew damp. 'He's passing on.' She pulled her beret down until her eyes were cast in shadow.

'Why'd you say that?' Derek asked worriedly.

'Coz you're changing.' Munkle pulled a mirror from her jumpsuit.

Derek took the mirror and stared into it. He was shocked at what he saw. The tuft of grey hair above his ear had grown considerably thicker and an identical clump had formed on the other side of his head.

'You're becomin' Santa,' Munkle continued, pointing at Derek's hair. 'That only happens when one Santa passes on and the next is preparing to take over. Your dressing gown is blue, right?'

'Yes,' Derek said, rather confused.

'Look at it now.'

Derek glanced down to see tiny flecks of pink in the material. Slowly, but surely, his dressing gown was changing colour.

Munkle gave him a sympathetic look. 'Soon you'll have the fuzzy beard, a podgy tum-tum, the scarlet suit, and long, curly white hair. The lot!'

'B-but I'm only s-seven,' Derek stammered.

'Don't matter,' Munkle added glumly. 'If Santa passes, you'll look eighty. The transformation is all part o' the magic of Christmas.'

Derek fell silent. What could he say? He wasn't ready to be Santa Claus. Not yet, anyway. And the thought of Santa Claus passing on – well, that was just the saddest thing he'd ever heard.

'Is there anything we can do?'

Derek asked desperately.

'No,' Munkle replied. 'Not unless we can find him and give him Elvun Dust.'

'What's Elvun dust?'

'It's magical dust. Only elves can make it. The dust is the source of all of Santa's power. It's the dust that makes the reindeers fly - that allows Santa to be able to deliver all the pressies in a single night. But here's the rub: only the true Santa Claus can make the dust magical. Elves can't do it. If only we could give him some Elvun Dust everything'd be hunky dory. And you could carry on as a normal kidder until you were old enough to take over.'

'Then we've got to find him,'

'We've been tryin',' Munkle replied sadly. 'We don't know where to look.'

A gloomy silence swept through the car. Derek became lost in his thoughts. Where was Santa? Who had taken him? And, as he glanced up at the carpet of twinkling stars above, he knew this wasn't just about saving Christmas anymore. It was, if at all possible, about saving Santa himself . . .

Chapter 3

The Rudolph Rocket

As the minutes raced by, Derek found himself becoming more and more anxious: How could he possibly be the new Santa Claus? How daft would he look with a belly the size of a cow? What on earth were his mum and dad going to say when he turned up on Boxing Day with a beard?

Every now and again he would look at Munkle who appeared increasingly nervous, making strange clicking sounds with her jaw and twiddling the pointy bit of her right ear between her fingers.

Then, suddenly, the aerocar began

to shudder. Derek's grip tightened around his scrunched up knees. He glanced anxiously at Munkle.

'Nowt to worry about, Derek,' Munkle said. 'We're slowin' down, preparing to land.'

The Sprite 1200 plunged through a particularly fluffy cloud. When they emerged on the other side, Derek was astounded to see a vast stretch of ice that coated the landscape like a silver table-cloth.

'The South Pole,' Munkle announced.

Derek watched as Munkle pressed a large purple button on the dashboard. Then she leaned over and pressed her mouth against what appeared to be a plastic snowman wobbling on a spring.

'Captain Elleana Munkle commencin' landing procedure ... Alert High Commissioner Krinkle …

Out and over.'

At once, a narrow crack appeared on the snowman's face. Then it began to talk. 'Okey mokey, Captain Munkle, park your vehicle in landing bay 28. Approach hatch opening ... Out and over.'

In the distance, Derek saw a tiny black speck plainly visible against the brilliant white. The further they dropped, the larger it grew until he saw an open door set into the ice. Munkle steered them through the hatch, and suddenly they swallowed by darkness.

When his eyes adjusted, Derek saw they were in a very long and winding tunnel. A few moments later, he saw light.

The Sprite 1200 slowed down all the time, until it travelled at the speed of a normal car. Derek suddenly felt much safer, and he looked ahead,

eager to see Poleland for the first time.
But as the Sprite 1200 moved towards
the light, the gravity of his situation
struck him. What was he doing here?
A big part of him wanted to plead
with Munkle to take him home
immediately. But before he could say
anything, the aerocar flew into an
enormous hangar the size of a football
pitch. There were more than two
dozen aerocars parked in various small
bays.

However, what really surprised him
were the hundreds of elves standing
on a wide platform beside the bays,
many of them holding large banners
that read, 'Poleland welcomes Derek
Brundle', 'Hello-ho-ho to the next
Santa' and 'The Elvand Little League
welcomes Derek Brundle.'

Derek couldn't take it all in. Then
he saw something even more
unexpected. Behind the crowd stood

a brown steam train with the words
'The Rudolph Rocket' painted on the
side; huge, wispy chunks of pink
smoke billowed from its funnel.

Munkle shook her head. 'Word
must have got out you were comin'.'
She landed the Sprite 1200, leaped out
and dashed to Derek's door. As
Munkle opened it, there was a
deafening burst of sound.

Elves were clapping and cheering
and whooping and stamping their feet.
As Derek stepped out, he was rushed
by dozens of very tiny elves, all eager
to touch him.

'Now, kidders, don't crowd him,'
Munkle said to the elf children. 'This
is a lot for him to take in. He's just a
kidder too, remember.'

Munkle's words were lost in a
chorus of excited squeals.

Derek couldn't help but return a
smile to the happy faces and he shook

as many of their little hands as he could. Then, as Munkle led him through the crowd, he caught sight of his dressing gown. It was entirely pink now. A wave of alarm rushed him and he seized Munkle's arm.

'Munkle, look…' he said, pointing to his gown.

Munkle nodded miserably. 'I know, Derek. We need to get you to the Town Hall. We need to see Krinkle.' She turned to the crowd and shouted, 'Let us through, please.'

The crowd parted, revealing a scarlet carpet that led to The Rudolph Rocket.

Up close, the train looked magnificent; a pink mist surrounded it where the smoke had settled in the air. As Derek walked up the carpet, a bit of smoke went into his mouth. Thinking he might cough, he was surprised to find it wasn't smoke at all.

'It's candyfloss!' Derek breathed.

Munkle smiled back. 'Yeppers, but don't eat too much. You won't want to eat the train.'

Derek looked shocked. 'Eat the train?'

'Yeppers,' Munkle said. 'Feel free to munch any bit you want.'

Derek looked up at the train, flabbergasted. Now that he was this close he could see it was indeed made from dark and milk and white chocolate. The wheels were made from thick liquorice and the funnel was made from something that resembled a gigantic walnut whip. He noticed that a carriage door was already open and Munkle led him in.

The moment the door closed, Derek felt a deep rumble from beneath and the train shuddered. Taking a moment to wave to the crowd outside, he watched as the air turned pink with candyfloss.

Derek turned to see that Munkle was sitting on a white sofa that lined the left hand side of the carriage. Then, quite unexpectedly, she grabbed a thick chunk of its arm rest and offered it to Derek.

'Here, Derek, 'ave some marshmallow.'

Derek took the marshmallow and threw it into his mouth; it glided down his throat, filling his body with a glorious feeling.

The Rudolph Rocket moved into a dimly lit tunnel, and as it emerged from the other side, Derek saw a gigantic city that stretched as far as the eye could see. Large schools painted in every colour imaginable, play parks that looked like fairgrounds, towering chimneys spouting green and violet smoke, enormous bright yellow factories, and row upon row of small, perfectly formed houses. He was also amazed to see more and more elves lining the track, many holding banners with his name on them.

After a few minutes, Derek could feel the Rudolph Rocket slow down. They were in the heart of the city now and surrounded by some very grand buildings indeed.

As the train drew to a halt, Derek saw the most magnificent building he'd ever seen. It looked very old and had dozens of steps that led to two huge wooden doors.

Munkle leapt up. 'Right, Derek. This is the Town Hall. I'll come in with you, but there'll be plenty o' brainier elves than me who will help you with what you have to do. Just 'member, I'll always be there for you if you need me.'

Derek suddenly felt very worried. He felt determined not to let anyone down and he knew he would do whatever he could. But as he followed Munkle up the stone steps, it struck him again: How on earth could he help save Christmas?

He was, after all, just a seven year old boy with grey hair and a pink dressing gown…

Chapter 4

The High Commissioner

Derek approached the great doors
with an uneasy feeling. The butterflies
in his belly felt like helicopters. Before
he reached the top step, however, the
doors opened and a very tiny figure
stood there, dressed in a long ruby
cloak that swept the floor. The lady
elf's face was old and lined with kind
eyes and long grey hair tied in a bun.
Derek watched as Munkle gave a very
deep bow. She bowed back. Then her
gaze fell on Derek.

'Hello-ho-ho, Derek. I'm Krinkle,
and may I welcome you to Poleland.'
Her voice was soft, warm and full of
the kind of confidence that comes
from living a very long time.

'Thank you very much.'

'Now, I'm sure Munkle has told you something of why you are here.'

'I told him everything,' Munkle added.

Krinkle sighed. 'I thought you might. Very well. Derek, you must be rather bewildered?'

'Yeah, a bit.'

The lady elf smiled warmly. 'Well, please come to my office and I'll explain everything.' She spun round and disappeared.

Derek and Munkle followed. They entered what was a grand marble hall with a colossal Christmas tree swathed in silver baubles set in the middle.

When Derek approached it, however, he was flabbergasted to see they weren't baubles at all; they were very small winged people that waved to him as he passed by. However, their wings hardly moved and their little faces looked rather glum.

'Bet you've never seen fairy lights made from real fairies, have you?' Munkle asked. 'Course, they're not on top form coz of what's happened to Santa.'

Derek nodded.

Krinkle stopped at a very striking golden door. 'This is the most important room in Poleland.' She pushed it open and they walked in.

Derek followed her into a vast room, its walls lined with dozens of clocks, each with the names of the countries of the world on them, all reading different times. There were hundreds of very unhappy looking elves sitting at computers, their work interrupted by regular bouts of sobbing and some very loud nose-blowing. Within seconds, however, you could hear a pin drop. The elves had stopped what they were doing and were looking wide-eyed at Derek. One by one, they stood, and bowed.

Derek was unsure of what to do, so he bowed back. The elves seemed to appreciate this and a great wail rang out as many started to sob again.

'Back to work, please, everyone,' Krinkle shouted, before turning back to Derek. 'We call this the Christmas Room. This is where we sort out all the deliveries for tomorrow. As you can see, everyone is rather upset. Everyone really loved this Santa...' Her voice quivered. 'He was...' A tear settled in her eye and she couldn't finish her sentence.

Derek didn't know what to say, so he placed his hand on hers. She calmed herself immediately. 'Would you come into my office?'

Derek followed Krinkle through a side door to a neat and tidy room with an oil painting of a distinguished looking elf wearing a turban hung on the left hand wall. Streams of silver and blue garlands hung from the ceiling and an elaborate wooden perch where six robins sat, chirping merrily, stood in the corner.

Krinkle sat down and pointed for Derek to do the same. 'First of all, Derek, I'm very sad you had to find out like this. We've never had to tell a manfolk kidder they're the next Santa Claus before.'

'Erm, that's okay,' Derek replied.

'Well, as Munkle has told you, the present Santa has been kidnapped. And we fear the worst, he's very old, you see – a hundred and fifty seven, to be precise.'

Derek gasped loudly. He had never heard of anyone living to that age before. 'How was he kidnapped?'

Krinkle sighed. 'He was walking his dogs, Crumpet and Marmalade, on the surface and judging by the footprints we found in the snow, was pounced on by four or five people.'

'But who would kidnap Father Christmas?'

'We don't know,' Krinkle replied. 'We've not heard from them. There have been no demands. All we know is that unless we can return him to Poleland in twelve hours, he will pass on.' Her bottom lip quivered. 'Oh dear ... Oh dear ...and he was such a wonderful Santa too ...' She began to cry.

'Please don't cry, Krinkle.' Derek pleaded. 'There's still time.'

Krinkle wiped her eyes with her sleeve. 'There really isn't, Derek. And unless we can get you to harness the power of the Elvun Dust, the world will have no Christmas.' Tears were falling thick and fast now. 'Oh, how awful... how very, very awful...'

Derek felt like giving her a hug, but she seemed so small and delicate he thought he might break her. Instead, he pulled his handkerchief from his gown pocket and passed it to her. 'Here, take this.'

Krinkle forced a smile and took it. 'Thank you.'

'How can I help?' Derek said.

Krinkle looked as though she was about to cry again, but stopped herself. 'Well, the first thing we must do is to give you Elvun Dust. You won't be as powerful as you will become when Santa passes on...' Her eyes started to leak again. 'But you will still possess some of the magic, and - '

There was a loud crash and the office door flew open. Standing there, struggling for breath, was an old, round elf with carroty hair, very fat legs and no neck. He held something in his right hand.

'Buntleflip … what is it?' Krinkle asked with concern.

The elf called Buntleflip looked up, his face red and sweaty. 'I've found summat, Ma'am,' he wheezed. 'Summat on the surface, near where Santa was nabbed!'

Krinkle's eyes widened. 'What do you mean?'

'Ere, Ma'am...' Buntleflip held out his right hand to reveal a large, black button with a 'D' in its centre. 'It was buried in the snow, near where the ol' fella went missin'.' It's a clue, Ma'am, innit?'

Krinkle's hand trembled as she took the button.

Munkle appeared at the door. 'What's up?'

Buntleflip struggled for breath. 'I've found summat, Captain Munkle. Fink it's a button. Fink it's off one of them that nicked Santa.'

Munkle's face shone with hope. 'Can I see it?'

Krinkle passed her the button.

'It's not much,' Munkle admitted, 'but we can check S.E.S databases. We might be able to find a match with –'

But then a quiet and rather shaky voice spoke up. 'May I see it?' Derek asked.

Seeing the strange expression on Derek's face, Munkle passed it over. Hardly daring to breathe, Derek turned the button in his fingers, his heart pounding. 'I've seen this 'D' sign before.'

The room fell silent. All eyes were on him.

For what seemed like an eternity, Derek studied the button, his brain desperately trying to remember where he had seen it.

And then, a few moments later, he did remember. But it didn't make sense. No sense at all.

Chapter 5
The Zoot Chute

'It's off a toy,' Derek said.

'What do you mean?' Munkle asked, puzzled.

Excitedly, Derek waved the button in the air. 'This is off a jacket of a Delta Man toy. I used to have one. Do you make them here?'

'No,' Krinkle said suspiciously. 'They're not one our brands.'

'Well, it definitely is,' Derek said. 'My mum and dad got me one last birthday. They're an action toy for kids and really expensive. Trouble was, it was a load of rubbish and fell apart after a week or so.' He looked at the button again. 'It's the 'D' that gives it away. I've never seen one this size before, though.'

Munkle shot Krinkle a very determined look. 'We need to get Derek and the button to S.E.S. Headquarters.'

Krinkle looked worried. 'But Derek needs to -'

'- to come with me,' Munkle finished. 'If there's any chance this button can lead us to Santa we've gotta take it.'

Krinkle hesitated for a second and then nodded. 'Very well.'

'Can we use your Zoot Chute?' Munkle asked.

'Of course,' Krinkle replied.

Derek looked confused. What was a Zoot Chute? He watched as Krinkle walked over to the portrait of the turban wearing elf. She pressed her left hand on the turban and the painting flipped round, revealing a round metal door behind.

'C'mon, Derek,' Munkle said urgently.

Derek leapt from his chair and followed Munkle to the door.

'You want me to come, Munkle?' Buntleflip asked. 'I used ter be pretty good if there were scrappin' t' be done.'

'No, Buntleflip. You stay with Krinkle. You've been top-elf today.'

Buntleflip's old face creased with pride.

Krinkle's hand moved over to a panel beside the door. Derek could see buttons labelled with dozens of room names. Her hand stopped at the one labelled 'S.E.S. HQ.' She pressed it. Suddenly, from behind the metal door, Derek heard the churning sound of metal grinding against metal.

'What's going on? Derek asked Munkle. 'What's a Zoot Chute?'

'Ah, you'll love it. It's a big slide. We can travel anywhere in Poleland from here, in no time at all.'

The grinding sound stopped. Munkle wrenched open the door handle exposing a pitch black tunnel. Derek's felt his hands dampen with sweat.

Then Krinkle spoke, desperation in her voice. 'Munkle, you can have Derek for one hour. But if he can't help he must be returned immediately.'

'I will,' Munkle said, climbing onto the door frame. 'May I have that, please, Derek?' She pointed to the Delta Man button. Derek passed it over. Thrusting the button in her pocket, she looked at Derek, who stared apprehensively at the hole. 'Now, there's nowt to worry about. I love the Zoot Chute and I've done it millions of times.' And with a

'Wheeeeeee!' she disappeared into blackness.

'Don't be scared, Derek.' Krinkle said. 'It's very safe. I'm a thousand and four years old and I love it.' She took his hand gently and guided it onto the rim. Derek pulled himself inside the hole, his hands clinging tightly to the edge.

'Just shut your eyes and enjoy the ride.' Krinkle said.

Then Derek let go.

At once, he sped down the tunnel. Up ...Down ... Faster and faster ... zipping this way and that ... *swish*, he turned a corner...*whoosh*, he turned another. It was better than any water slide. A few moments later, he saw a speck of light in the distance. And he was slowing down. More light. Slower, still. He clamped his eyes shut.

Then, to his horror, he felt nothing beneath him ... he was flying through the air … and - *poofff* - he landed on something … something soft, like a bouncy castle. Catching his breath, he opened his eyes to see Munkle stood there, hands on hips.

'Now, wasn't that great,' she said, grinning.

'Yeah,' Derek gushed. 'Can we do it again?'

'Not now,' Munkle said. 'We've got work to do.' And she helped Derek off the landing cushion.

Derek looked around at a technical looking room, coloured in dark greens and purples. There were tall banks of computer workstations, red and yellow filing cabinets and a large pink sign that read 'Special Elf Service – Who Cares Wins.' However, the most unusual object sat in the middle of the room: an old fashioned fruit machine decorated in thick blue tinsel and a floppy Santa hat.

Then he realised he was being watched.

Three elves stared at him. The elf on the left was the tallest he had seen and had a beetroot nose. The female elf standing in the middle was small and pretty with raven-black hair and emerald eyes. But it was the elf on the right that caught his eye. He was nearly as wide as he was tall and looked like a washing machine.

'Hello,' Derek said.

The elves said nothing.

'Now, Team,' Munkle said, 'that's no way to greet the new Santa.'

Still overcome with shock, the three elves glanced at each other. The girl elf led the way and bowed. A second later, the other elves bowed too.

Derek, let me introduce you to my colleagues,' Munkle said. 'This is Spitch.' He pointed to the tall elf.

'Greta.' He pointed to the female elf.
'And this stocky dippy doughnut is
Lock.'

One by one, Derek shook their
hands and introduced himself.

'What's goin' on, Munkle?' Spitch
asked, bewildered.

'Buntleflip found summat on the
surface. Think it's from one of the
nappers. Derek thinks it's from a manfolk toy. It may lead us to Santa.'

The elves looked at each other with
amazement.

'Ere, Spitch.' Munkle threw him
the button. 'Load it into Ernie, will
you?'

Derek watched as Spitch ran to the
fruit machine. He slotted the button
into it and pulled a golden handle.
Suddenly, a fat beam of light gushed
from top of the machine and filled the
room. Derek looked up and saw a
giant image of the button that turned

and flipped in the air.

Munkle saw the disbelief on Derek's face. 'Ernie is one of the most powerful computers in Poleland, Derek. In short, he knows everything.'

Then Ernie began to speak. 'I am rather fantastic, Agent Munkle, thank you for noticing.'

Munkle leaned over to Derek. 'Oh, and he's a right big-head.'

Derek grinned.

'Ernie,' Munkle continued. 'Can you show me if the button fits the uniform of a toy called the Delta Man?'

A second later, a Delta Man figure appeared beside the button. The button then shrunk and slotted onto the figure's jacket. It was a perfect fit.

A gasp of astonishment echoed through the room.

Munkle drew a deep breath. 'Ernie, can you tell me which company makes the Delta Man?'

'Certainly, I can do anything,' Ernie replied. 'I'm great!'

'Get on with it,' Munkle growled.

The Delta Man disappeared and a company logo stood in its place. 'Horridge Enterprises,' Ernie said.

Munkle's face drained of colour. 'I might've guessed.'

Derek noticed. 'What is it, Munkle?'

Munkle seemed not to hear him. 'Upload all information on Charles Horridge.'

'Who's Charles Horridge?' Derek asked.

'He's a toy-maker,' Munkle said. 'He owns the biggest man-folk toy company in the world. A genius, so they say, but a terrible man – only ever been on the naughty boy list. And his sales have plummeted lately. Seems like no one wants to buy his overpriced junk.'

Suddenly Derek was looking up at a face, a very thin and bony face with dull grey eyes and a thin, black, pointy beard. 'And do you think he's kidnapped Santa?'

'Well, he's got the means and the money. But he's a recluse. No one in his company has seen him for years. He just lives alone in his castle off the coast of Scotland and controls everything from there.'

But Derek had stopped listening. 'He lives in a castle?'

'Yeppers,' Munkle said.

'Have you got a picture of it?'

'Ernie, have you got a piccy of Horridge Castle?'

As an image of a sinister looking castle floated before them, Derek turned pale. 'I've seen it before,' he breathed.

Munkle looked back at him,

confused. 'You've seen Horridge Castle?'

'Yes,' Derek said. 'This morning, in a dream. A really life-like dream. I was being dragged through the castle by someone I couldn't see.'

'You were dragged?' Munkle asked curiously.

'Yes,' Derek replied. 'He's there. Santa's in that castle. I know he is. He's in the dungeons. Somehow, Santa must have used some magic or something to send the images into my head.' He took a deep breath. 'We have to go there. We can save him!'

Munkle said nothing. She looked at Spitch, then Greta and finally Lock; each of them looked like they had swallowed a toilet brush.

Seconds passed.

And then Munkle nodded. 'Maybe we can…'

Derek felt his heart rush with joy.

They were going to rescue Santa Claus.

Chapter 6

The Elvun Dust

Munkle moved with squirrel-like speed. 'Okey mokey, Team… Spitch, you're in charge of weapons - we'll need three full assault kits: Fudgebusters, Water Bombs, Strawberry Shoelaces, Hover-shoes, and a Bungle Cannon. Oh, and type in the castle's position on the Paragumblies, will you? ' Spitch nodded and ran through a door on the right. 'Greta, prepare the Terrier Elf-jet 3001 for immediate take-off.' Greta nodded and ran though a door on the left. Then she turned to Lock. 'You just eat a dozen mince cakes and keep your strength up. Lock stomped through a door in the middle.

'What do you want me to do?' Derek asked.

Munkle smiled affectionately. 'I want you to stay with Krinkle. This mission might not work remember.'

'But I have to go,' Derek insisted.

'You don't,' Munkle replied, pulling a walkie-talkie from her pocket.'

'I do,' Derek pressed. 'I know where Santa Claus is, remember. I've seen inside that castle. I know how to get to the dungeons. Time is running out and I'm the quickest way to find him.'

It was obvious in her haste, Munkle hadn't considered that. 'But – but it might be dangerous.'

'Danger's my middle name,' Derek said bravely.

'Your middle name's Nigel,' Munkle added. 'Don't forget we know everything about you.'

Derek frowned, and in his most stubborn voice said, 'I'm still coming.'

Munkle mulled this over for a few seconds, as if struggling to find a counter argument. She didn't have one. 'Okey mokey. But I'm gonna get in a heap load of troll trollop if anything happens to you.' She raised the walkie-talkie. 'Krinkle?'

Derek watched as the walkie-talkie's screen lit up and Krinkle's face appeared, looking troubled. 'Munkle … have you found anything? Is Derek okay?'

'Derek's tickety boo, Ma'am. And yes, we've found something. In fact, we think we know who's got Santa and where he is. It's Charles Horridge – you know, the toymaker.'

'I have heard of him,' Krinkle muttered sourly.

'We're making preparations,' Munkle continued, 'and we're going to

Horridge's Castle in Scotland as soon as we can.'

'Good,' Krinkle said.

Munkle looked awkward. 'And er, well, er, Derek's coming with us. He's, er, going to be part o' the rescue team.'

There was a brief silence, and then Munkle's entire body seemed to shrink. Even with her hand over the receiver, Derek could hear Krinkle shouting very loudly. Every now and again, he heard words like 'Flinking Blidiot,' Troll-dudgebrain', 'Ringle Natstoad' and 'Bufferoon' - and although he didn't know what they meant, he felt certain they weren't very nice.

Derek knew Krinkle must have hung up because Munkle put the walkie-talkie back in her pocket and frowned.

'Ooops,' she said, smiling weakly.

'Ol' Krinkly's not best pleased.'

Derek nodded, when suddenly he heard a curious sound coming from the Zoot Chute. It grew louder and, seconds later, a robed figure soared through the air and landed on the cushion. Krinkle leapt off with the speed of someone much younger than her years.

'Er, hello-ho-ho again, Ma'am,' Munkle said timidly.

Krinkle's face grew strawberry red. 'Don't give me any of your flabber. What are you thinking, Munkle?'

Munkle struggled to find any words. 'It, err, it -'

'It was my idea, Krinkle,' Derek said calmly. 'I want to go. I have to go. I had a dream, you see, and in the dream I was being led through Horridge's Castle to a dungeon. Santa must have used what little bit of magic he'd got left to send me his position. I can help…'

Krinkle was lost for words. She groaned and after a few moments, her body deflated like a popped balloon. 'I suppose you're right, Derek.'

'Course, he is,' Munkle said cheerily, desperately trying to get back into Krinkle's good books. It didn't work.

Krinkle gave her the nastiest of looks then turned back to Derek. 'Well, I suppose if you are going we'd better make sure you're prepared.' She rummaged through her pockets and removed a velvet pouch with a leather strap. She opened it and pulled something out.

'This is Elvun Dust,' Krinkle said. 'Shall we try it out?'

Looking nervously at the dust, Derek nodded and watched as Krinkle sprinkled a few grains on his head.

For a moment, he felt nothing. But

then a curious thing happened. His fingers tingled, his nose shivered and a strange feeling swept through his body. It was wonderful. He felt like he could do anything.

'Can you feel it?' Krinkle asked.

A wide smile curled on Derek's mouth. 'Yes. What can I do?'

Krinkle smiled. 'Whatever you want, my dear. You have the power of Christmas now. Think of something, and if you concentrate hard enough, you can do it.'

Slowly, Derek turned to Munkle and closed his eyes.

'Oi, what are you -?' But before Munkle could finish, she had risen off the floor and was floating like a feather on a breeze.

'See, Derek,' Krinkle said.

Derek forced his eyes open. He gasped loudly as he watched Munkle pass in front of him, her little legs waving madly.

Munkle giggled. 'Oi, Derek, put me down.'

Derek did so at once. 'What else can I do?'

'I told you,' Krinkle said. 'Anything.'

'Can I fly?' Derek said.

'Of course,' Krinkle said. 'But I wouldn't. Flying takes quite a lot of Elvun Dust and you are going to need to save as much of it as you can if you're going to rescue Santa and bring him safely back here.' She curled the pouch over his neck. 'Now, you mustn't waste it. It's very rare.'

'I won't,' Derek replied. He smiled at Krinkle, but was shocked to see she her frowning at him. He glanced over at Munkle, who also looked very worried.

'What is it?' Derek asked anxiously.

Munkle gulped. 'Ernie, can you

show me a mirror?'

'Course I can,' the fruit machine replied. 'I'm remarkable.'

A beam of light shot out of Ernie and formed a very solid looking mirror. Softly, Munkle took Derek's arm and stood him in front of it.

Derek felt his mouth go dry. He could barely recognise himself. His robe was now entirely red and his belt was a brilliant white. But it was his hair that shocked him the most. It was now completely silver, there wasn't a single patch of black left.

Then his heart sank further. Poking through his chin, like thin blades of grass, were very noticeable bristles of the deepest grey.

He was growing a beard.

Chapter 7

The Terrier Elf-Jet

Derek felt awful. Any joy he'd felt at having special powers instantly disappeared. He was a seven year old boy with grey hair and a beard - a freak - someone to be pointed at in the street and laughed at, like his teacher, Mr Twimble, who had a head like a coconut.

Hesitantly, he pressed his fingers against his chin. It was rough and prickly like sandpaper. For the next few minutes he said nothing and paced anxiously around the room trying to avoid anything that cast a reflection. Then Krinkle walked over and took his hand.

'I know this has come as a shock,' she said softly, 'but the hair, the beard, the weight, it's all temporary. They appear on Christmas Eve and disappear by Boxing Day ... the rest of the year you will look completely normal.'

'Really?'

'Really.'

Her words made him feel better. But then something else struck him. 'When I'm Santa will I have to stay in Poleland? Forever, I mean, and not see my family or my friends ever again.'

Krinkle smiled. 'Not at all, Derek. You can live a normal life, if you wish. Santa is only really needed for the two days at Christmas. The rest of the year the elves make the toys and the other presents. You would just come here to deliver them. And there's something else…' Krinkle hesitated. 'You don't even have to be Santa unless you really want to be. If you refuse, the magic will simply transfer to someone else. I think the question you have to ask yourself is: do I want to be the next Santa Claus?'

Derek felt winded. He didn't have to be Santa Claus? He could let someone else do the job. He found himself thinking very hard, about everything Santa stood for, all the happiness felt by people everywhere as they opened their presents on Christmas morning, the smiles as they sang their favourite carols. And then it struck him: Christmas stood for goodness. And, although he was only seven, he knew there wasn't enough goodness in the world. How could he not want to be a part of that? The conclusion he came to was very clear.

'Yes. I do,' he said softly. 'More

than anything.'

Krinkle placed her hand gently on his shoulder. 'That's good. I am pleased.'

Suddenly the right hand door flew open. Spitch entered, followed by Lock, who had a fat chunk of mince cake hanging from his bottom lip.

'You got everything?' Munkle asked.

'Aye, Captain,' Spitch replied. 'Everything's loaded. Greta's just refuelling and we're ready to rumble, ain't we Lock?'

Lock nodded and a lump of pastry fell to the floor.

A minute later, they were stood beside the Zoot Chute. Derek felt rather nervous now and kept fiddling with the Elvun Dust pouch. Krinkle looked like she was about to cry again.

Derek reached over and took her hand. 'We'll be fine, Krinkle.'

Her eyes reddened. 'You're a brave boy, Derek. I just know you'll make a wonderful Santa one day.'

Munkle moved forward. 'I'll take care of him, Ma'am. And whatever happens, even if ...' she struggled to find the words, 'even if we can't save our Santa, I promise I'll have him back in time. Christmas will happen, and it will happen tomorrow.'

'Thank you, Munkle,' Krinkle said, her voice quivering.

Derek watched as Munkle's hand hovered over the wall panel beside the Zoot Chute. She pressed a button that read 'Terrier Elf-Jet Hangar.' A recognisable sound of grinding metal rang out as the Zoot Chute changed position. Then Munkle opened the hatch and, one by one, the elves leapt into the hole, until only Krinkle and Derek remained.

'Good luck, Derek,' Krinkle said,

and she gave him the strongest hug she could manage. Derek hugged her back, and then he, too, disappeared into the hole.

This time Derek closed his eyes. Speeding through the Zoot Chute didn't seem as much fun. His mind was elsewhere. He was going on a mission, and a potentially dangerous one at that. Was he ready for it? But before he had time to answer his own question, he found himself flying through the air again, before landing softly on what he assumed was another cushion.

Opening his eyes, he saw he was in an aircraft hangar. However, for once, there were no breathtaking Christmas decorations, no bright, wonderful colours. The room was very different from everything else he had seen in Poleland.

Hearing movement to his left, he

turned and his eyes nearly popped from his head. He'd assumed they would be flying in a jet-plane. Or at least something that resembled a jet-plane. Instead, he found himself gawping, wide-eyed, at a red ice cream with a white, shaggy dog wearing flying goggles and a leather jacket painted on the side. Next to it, in bright golden letters, were the words 'The Terrier Elf-jet 3001.' Munkle helped him off the cushion and together they approached the van.

'The Terrier Elf-jet's totally state of the art,' Munkle said. 'There ain't nowt like her in the manfolk world, either. Makes the Sprite 1200 look like a go-kart.'

Derek saw a head appear on the driver's side.

'All fuelled up, Captain Munkle,' Greta shouted.

'Thank you, Greta.' She turned to

Derek. 'Greta is the finest pilot in the Special Elf Service. Best there's ever been ...'

Greta smiled proudly.

Then Munkle's face turned grave. 'Now, let's haul bum bums … We've got one very poorly Santa to rescue...'

Munkle, Spitch, Lock and finally Derek, climbed aboard the ice cream van. Inside, Derek saw stacks of blinking buttons, dials of all shapes and sizes, screens with multi-coloured lights flashing, and lots of other very technical looking equipment. There were also three black rucksacks laid out carefully on the floor. His eyes widened.

Next to the packs were what looked like three toy water rifles; two were small, thin and made from yellow plastic and clear tubing; the other, however, was long, fat and as black as coal.

Munkle and Spitch each picked up a yellow rifle.

'This is a Fudgebuster,' Munkle said to Derek. 'It's a stun gun. Can't hurt anything, but hit someone and they'll instantly freeze like an ice statue.'

Derek watched Lock pick up the black rifle. It was very nearly as big as he was.

'That's a Bungle Cannon,' Munkle said. 'Only Lock's strong enuff to carry that one. One blast from that can blow a hole in a mountain.'

Derek watched as the elves slung their back packs on and pulled belts across their chests. Derek did the same.

There was a loud high-pitched sound. The Elf-jet began to shake. The sound grew louder. Derek felt his stomach jolt. The ice cream van had risen a foot or so from the ground.

Nervously, Derek glanced at Munkle.

'Here we go…' Munkle said.

The noise grew. The van seemed to hover for a second, suspended in the air like a bird of prey, then – BOOM – they were off. Derek could feel pressure squash his chest, his cheeks wobbled like jelly. The ice cream van sliced the air at a mindboggling speed.

A second later they hurtled out of the hangar into a colourless sky. Higher and higher they flew, bursting through the murky clouds into the light above. The elf-jet levelled off.

Munkle looked at Derek and grinned. 'We should be there in about half an hour.'

Derek gave an uneasy nod. Then something rather heartening occurred to him. They were heading back to Britain.

He was going home.

Chapter 8

Horridge Castle

As the minutes raced by, a nervous silence flooded the van. Derek watched Munkle, Spitch and Lock closely, their faces growing more and more anxious. Then he noticed something else, something that made him feel even worse. Looking down, he saw his tummy stretching the material of his bright red gown. He was getting fatter. Much fatter. How depressing!

And so, for the next twenty minutes, he made a great deal of effort to think about nice things: playing football, eating cheesecake, and drinking iced lemonade on a hot summers day - anything to stop himself feeling miserable. Infact, he was thinking so hard about happy thoughts he didn't notice the ice cream van slow down.

He was jolted back to reality by Munkle, who stood up and checked the straps on her back pack. Spitch and Lock did the same. Then each of them picked up a rifle.

'Are we getting ready to land?' Derek asked.

'Land, Derek?' Munkle gave a weak smile. 'We're not landing…'

Derek looked confused. 'Then how are we going to - '

Anticipating Derek's question, Munkle said. 'We're going to use Paragumblies.' She looked guilty. 'Sorry, for not telling you. I figured it might add to your worry.'

Derek's face turned white. 'What's a paragumbly?' he asked, although he just knew very well he wouldn't like the answer.

'It's a parachute made from indestructible bubble gum.' Seeing Derek's horrified expression, she added, 'It's perfectly safe.'

'Yes, but I haven't -' Derek blustered. '- I haven't got a paragumbly.'

'You don't need one,' Munkle said. 'You're gonna to hold on t' me … here Spitch, take my Fudgebuster, will you?' Munkle passed the rifle over.

'What are you talking about? You're not strong enough to hold me.' Derek pulled open his robe to show off his bulging tummy. 'Look… I'm getting the Santa belly!'

Munkle didn't look quite as confident as she had a second before. Still, she drew a deep breath and said. 'Ah, I'm stronger than you think.'

'I'm not doing it!' Derek said

stubbornly.

'Fraid we have to, Derek.' Munkle shrugged. 'It's all about the element of surprise, you see? We can't just land an ice cream van in Horridge's back yard and knock on his door.'

'Well … I …err … I…' Derek couldn't find an answer.

'Exactly,' Munkle said. 'You're gonna to 'ave to trust me. Spitch has set the paragumblies to land on the castle walls, so we're quite safe.'

But Derek didn't feel safe. In fact, he felt as far from safe as it was possible to get. For one thing, Munkle was much smaller than he was. How on earth could Munkle handle his weight, particularly as he was getting heavier all the time? His concern grew when he heard Greta's voice. She sounded close to tears.

'Hatch doors will be opening in thirty seconds. Be careful down there and good luck…' She sniffed loudly. 'Elf kind and Man-folk are relying on you…'

Hearing the pain in her voice, Derek's fears disappeared. This was all about saving Santa Claus. The world needed him to be brave.

'Thanks, Agent Greta!' Spitch said. Lock grunted loudly.

Munkle turned to Derek. 'It will be safe. I promise.'

Derek was about to reply when a strange sound echoed from the rear of the van. The doors were opening. A blast of ice cold air struck his face. A moment later, Spitch and Lock jumped. He watched them disappear from sight and gulped. He couldn't follow them, could he? In the end, he didn't have a say in the matter.

'Sorry, Derek …' Munkle pushed him out of the van.

Derek was falling and falling fast.

He couldn't breathe … his arms thrashed madly. And Munkle was nowhere to be seen. Had she followed him out of the van? He squeezed his eyes shut….he was dead! …he knew it. But, suddenly, he felt arms around his waist.

'Fancy seeing you here,' Munkle grinned.

And then – WHOOSH – Derek wasn't falling anymore. He was flying upwards. He looked up to see an enormous umbrella of pink had opened above. The paragumbly had worked. He was dropping again, but slowly, gently this time.

Drifting through the air, he could see it was a very damp and hazy day. And he could see the sea now. It was everywhere, wild and brutal. He could see an island too. He looked over and, through the mist, saw Spitch and Lock in front of them. They were all safe.

Closer and closer they moved towards the island. He could see the crashing waves below. If he fell, he'd be drowned, for sure. But he wasn't about to fall. Munkle was stronger than she looked.

And then he spied it: Horridge Castle. It was the same castle from his dream, but if it looked creepy then, it looked positively frightening in real life.

They were nearly on the castle walls now. Derek saw six huge towers that sliced the sky. One, in particular, was taller and grander than the others with light filtering out from its topmost window.

Lower and lower they dropped. Then, finally, they touched down on hard stone.

'Wowza!' Munkle exclaimed. 'That was fun.'

Derek couldn't agree. Being

pushed from a flying ice cream van wasn't his idea of a good time. He watched as the Paragumbly shrunk into Munkle's back pack. Then he turned to look at his bleak surroundings. Considering it was Christmas Eve, he thought it must be the least Christmassy place on earth.

'D'you recognise it, Derek?' Munkle asked.

'Yes,' Derek replied. 'It's that way.' He pointed to a sturdy looking oak door on the far wall.

Munkle took her Fudgebuster from Spitch, and led the way. Standing beside the door, she tried the handle. It was locked. 'Do what you do best, Locky boy.'

Lock grunted, raised the Bungle Cannon and took aim.

'Stand back and cover your ears, Derek,' Munkle said.

Lock fired… KABOOM … the

door shattered into a million tiny pieces. Dust and smoke and splinters filled the air. Once the cloud settled, Derek saw a gaping space, revealing a long corridor behind. The high walls were lined with flaming torches that shed an orange glow over the dull grey walls. Munkle moved cautiously inside. Lock, Spitch and Derek followed.

Derek recognised the corridor at once. This was definitely the way Santa had entered the castle. His heart raced as they made their way down the passageway, each of them looking for the first sign of danger. But it was quiet. Deathly quiet.

But then a clang rang out behind them. Terrified, Derek's head turned. A thick steel plate had dropped from the ceiling and covered the doorway. They were sealed in, trapped. Then he glanced up to see speakers and cameras fixed to the ceiling. His heart plummeted when he heard a high-pitched, sneering voice. The ugliest voice he had ever heard.

'Good afternoon, little people. I'm so glad you could join me for my Christmas party. I just know we are going to have oodles of fun ...'

Chapter 9

Ant Attack

'Allow me to introduce myself,' the voice continued. 'I'm Charles Horridge – toymaker extraordinaire. I've been expecting you. I'm very aware how clever your little Special Elf Service is and it is pleases me that -' The voice stopped in its tracks.

Derek looked at Munkle with horror. What was going on?

Then laughter surrounded them, horrible, hideous laughter. 'Oh, how very delightful … You're not all elves, are you?' The laughter continued.' Surely, you haven't brought … I'm right, aren't I? You've brought the next Santa Claus with you. And unless, I'm mistaken, it's a boy! What a stroke of luck. Not only can I stop Christmas, but I can kill two birds with one stone, or at least two Santas in one day. Oh, this is wonderful…'

Munkle's face shone with fury. 'Horridge! You bumflapper! You just wait 'til I get my mittsys on you -'

Horridge cut in. 'I'm afraid that won't be happening, Captain Elleana Munkle.' His voice sounded particularly smug. 'Oh, yes, I am familiar with you and your little friends. I am, however, afraid there's no way you will be getting your 'mittsys' on me or, indeed, leaving this castle.' Horridge began to cackle again. 'You will find I have prepared a number of special surprises of my own devising, just for you. And I am certain you will not see another Christmas Day. But then, neither will the rest of the world…'

Then all fell silent.

Derek's stomach turned. He glanced at the elves. Their faces told him they were thinking the same as him: What did Charles Horridge mean by 'special surprises'?

Suddenly, a loud tapping sound cut the air. It was coming from the staircase. Munkle raised her Fudgebuster. Spitch did the same. Lock heaved the Bungle Cannon to his shoulder and took aim.

Derek looked ahead and his blood turned cold. Slowly, out of the shadows, came a huge black head with two curved pincers that twitched and clicked, followed by a thin dark brown body and six long spindly legs. It was a gigantic ant, the size of an Alsatian dog. The ant stopped and its swollen black eyes seemed to study them closely. Derek looked on in horror as eight other ants followed it into the corridor.

Time seemed to stop. A terrifying silence fell over the corridor. Then Derek heard Munkle shout: 'STAY BACK, DEREK!'

Suddenly, it was mayhem.

KABOOM! Lock fired the Bungle Cannon. The first ant exploded in a shower of metal and plastic. Derek realised it at once: they were toys. Giant, deadly toys.

The ants attacked. Some of them scaled the walls, some the ceiling - all were scurrying towards the elves, their hideous mouths open wide.

Munkle fired the Fudgebuster at the ant closest to her. BAM! A direct hit. The ant froze instantly. She fired again, hitting one on right hand wall.

Spitch fired too - another direct hit.

Lock fired at the ceiling. KABOOM! Two more ants exploded. Smoke was everywhere. Then, through the haze, an ant leapt through the air. Munkle fired, but missed. The ant landed on Spitch, knocking him to the floor. It pinned him down with its long legs. Spitch looked up in terror, when – BAM - the ant froze. Munkle had hit it full on. Spitch threw it off and clambered to his feet.

There were only two ants left now. They ran at the group. But Munkle and Spitch were too quick; each fired a single shot, each shot hit its target. The ants were as motionless as statues.

The attack was over. All was still.

Derek felt disorientated, relieved, but most of all, angry at himself. He'd panicked and forgot about the Elvun Dust. He hadn't done a thing to help.

Munkle walked over to him. 'Are you okay, Derek?'

Derek nodded weakly. Munkle turned to Lock and Spitch. 'Well done, soldiers. Good work!' Lock gave a satisfied grin.

Spitch looked visibly shaken. 'And to you, Captain.'

'We'd better get going,' Munkle said urgently.

Everyone agreed. Carefully weaving through the mass of frozen ants, the group walked to the end of the corridor, turned left, and down the staircase.

Derek did his best to hide the dread that swelled inside. Charles Horridge had sounded so confident they wouldn't leave the castle alive, and, taking a final, chilling glance at the motionless ants, Derek could understand why. But what other surprises had Horridge got planned for them?

Chapter 10

The Delta Men

They moved swiftly down the staircase, Derek leading the way, taking the steps two at a time. There was no sound except for the clap of footsteps echoing against stone.

'Is this the right way?' Munkle asked, her little legs struggling to keep up.

'Yes,' Derek replied. 'There's a Banquet Hall just down here. We need to go through the far door to get to the dungeons.'

Moments later, they were at the bottom of the staircase and facing another thick wooden door. Derek shivered with dread. Just as he was about to open it, he felt a tug on his arm. Munkle pulled him back, her Fudgebuster raised. She pulled at the door handle. It was unlocked. Slowly, she pushed the door open. It creaked loudly.

Derek felt a lump in his throat. Could Horridge have planned another deadly surprise for them inside? Peering in, he was relieved to see that all seemed quiet and still.

They entered the Banquet Hall. A huge room with a high and ornate ceiling, it had a long wooden table in the centre and a staircase that led to a gallery above. There were also what must have been twenty gleaming suits of medieval armour that lined the walls like frozen guards.

At the far end of the Hall, Derek could see the door. Excitement swept through him. They were close now.

But, suddenly, a loud bang from the gallery above rang out. A door had

burst open. Derek's heart sank.
Looking up, he saw a dozen armed
men march out, their identical plastic
faces cold and lifeless.

The men lined out in single file
against the balcony, like pieces on a
chessboard. Derek's heart sank further
when he saw their black and yellow
uniforms. Delta Men. Of course, he
had only ever seen Delta Men action
figures, but these weren't toys, these
were adult-sized Delta Men, and they
were ready for battle.

The elves looked helplessly at each
other. They were outnumbered four
to one. Still, they raised their weapons
and nodded silently at each other.
They weren't going down without a
fight.

At once, Charles Horridge's voice
filled the hall. 'DELTA MEN…
PREPARE FOR BATTLE!' With an
echoing clack, they hoisted their rifles

to their shoulders.

In that split second, Munkle shouted, 'TAKE COVER!' and the group sprinted to the table. Dropping to their knees, they slid beneath it.

Horridge continued. 'DELTA MEN ... KILL THE INTRUDERS.'

At once, an avalanche of noise shattered the stillness as bullets ripped into the table. Derek knew they were in trouble now. How on earth could three elves and a boy defeat twelve Delta Men with real guns?

Then it struck him: the Elvun Dust.

Derek pulled the pouch over his head. Desperately trying to keep his trembling hands steady, he untied it and pulled it open. He grabbed a pinch of dust and sprinkled it over his head. A split second later, he felt his nose quiver and a cooling sensation tickled his spine, as if someone had dropped an ice cube down his pyjamas. The magic was working.

Derek quickly glanced around the room, looking for a way to defeat the Delta Men. But how? And then, as if a light bulb had been switched on in his head, he knew what to do.

He had a plan.

Shutting his eyes, he concentrated with all his might. Pressure swamped his head, his brain felt like it might explode. Then a strange feeling coated his body - a beautiful feeling. He opened his eyes again to see if it had worked.

It had.

The suits of armour had come to life; each suit stepped forward and turned to the staircase. One by one, with a rhythmic clank, they moved steadily up to the gallery. The Delta Men saw this and turned on their new foe. They fired. The bullets tore through the armour, but proved useless. It was the Delta Men's turn to be outnumbered.

The suits of armour attacked. There were loud clangs and clanks as metal clashed with metal. Delta Men were pitched over the banister, shattering in pieces on the stone floor below.

'Well done, Derek. Brilliant stuff!' Munkle shouted, as she watched the scene above. 'Let's make a run for that door.'

So they ran.

Even with the extra weight, Derek reached the door first. Breathless, he flung it open and raced through. Munkle, Spitch and Lock followed him. Slamming the door shut, they saw another flight of steps that trailed below. Excitedly, they rushed to them, hoping against hope Horridge hadn't prepared anything else. They had, after all, surely not been expected to defeat giant killer ants and a dozen fully armed Delta Men?

Derek felt the temperature drop as they raced down the stairs. The further they ran, however, the more a very odd noise lingered on the musty air, like a heavy gust of blustery wind.

As Derek reached the final step, the sound was everywhere. Hesitantly, he turned the corner and fear ripped his body. He had found the source of the noise.

A colossal dragon lay curled into a ball directly before the dungeon's door. It was fast asleep and snoring as loudly as a foghorn.

Charles Horridge *had* prepared for all eventualities.

Chapter 11
The Dragon's Den

A stunned silence echoed through the cave. Then Derek spoke in his softest whisper. 'That's not – not a real dragon, is it? I mean, it's just another one of Horridge's toys, right?'

'I don't think it matters,' Munkle whispered back. 'It's big. It's nasty. And I think we're the turkey in its Christmas dinner. Toy or not!'

Derek wanted to run. But to where? They couldn't go back on themselves - there was a battle raging upstairs - and besides, Santa was close now. One way or another, they had to get into the dungeons.

Munkle looked around and saw the cavern was lined with dozens of small caves with entrances no more than a few feet wide. 'We should get to those caves, we'll be safe and can plan our next move ...' But just as the words left Munkle's mouth, the snoring stopped.

Every muscle in Derek's body turned to jelly. He watched helplessly as two eyelids opened. A pair of blood-red eyes watched them furiously. Slowly, the dragon climbed to its feet, its long, whip-like tail thrashing from side to side.

'W-what are we going t-to d-do?' Derek stuttered to Munkle in what could only be described as a shrill squeak.

Munkle stood upright as though about to do something very brave. Instead, she yelled, 'SCARPER...' and sprinted off in the direction of the caves. A split second later, Derek, Spitch and Lock raced after her. The dragon let out a thunderous roar and a bolt of fire shot from its mouth, narrowly missing Derek.

Feeling a blast of heat, he ran for all he was worth, the extra weight feeling like a tyre round his middle. He was close to the cave now. He watched Munkle leap through the cave entrance into blackness. The dragon took a rasping breath, preparing a second strike.

Knowing he would soon resemble crispy bacon if he didn't act, Derek launched himself into the air and flew into the cave, landing with a very heavy thump on the ground. A split second later, Spitch and Lock followed him into the cave.

Munkle dusted herself down and smiled feebly at the others. 'Right, err… I reckon it's safe to say Fudgebusters ain't gonna work on Mr Great Balls o' Fire.' Spitch and Lock nodded their agreement. 'The Bungle Cannon might do a bit of damage, but not enough.' She sighed. 'So how do we beat it?'

Silence.

After what seemed like an age, Spitch spoke, 'Er, if Derek turned the dragon into a pizza, Lock could eat it...'

'A pizza? Of all the stupidest ideas you could 'ave come up with, troll-brain,' Munkle said, much to Spitch's dismay. Then she shot him a wide grin. 'I love it. Derek, you reckon you turn ol' flame-breath into a deep pan Pepperoni?'

'I don't know. It's enormous,' Derek admitted. 'How much dust will that take?'

'Dunno,' Munkle shrugged. 'How much you got left?'

Derek opened his pouch.

Munkle frowned. 'There's enough. Just not sure there's enough to get Santa back to full health after you've done it.'

The group's mood turned from hopeful to glum.

'What else have you got in your assault kit?' Derek asked.

Munkle opened her back pack and started to pull out various items.

Derek recognised the first object.

'Hover-shoes,' Munkle said, placing them carefully on the floor. Then she took out what looked like a red yoyo. 'This is a strawberry shoe-lace - strongest cord known to elfkind.' And finally she pulled out a small, round plastic bottle with bright green liquid swirling inside. 'And this is a water-bomb.'

Derek's face dropped. It really wasn't much of a bomb and would clearly be useless against a robot dragon.

Munkle noted the disappointment on Derek's face. 'It's not just any old water-bomb, you know …' She held it up into the light. 'This bottle contains Stretchy water. Once the shell is broken, the water expands until there's enuff to fill a small lake.'

Derek did a double take. Stretchy water? Then he suddenly had the most marvellous idea. 'That's it!' he exclaimed.

'What is it?' Munkle asked.

'How to beat the dragon,' Derek said excitedly. 'It's a toy, right, with lots of electronic circuits and batteries and stuff. Surely, if we can get the dragon to swallow the bomb the water will damage its parts, like dropping a mobile phone in a bath.' Munkle looked impressed. 'And I'll use magic to make sure the bomb gets into the dragon's mouth. That won't use up much Elvun dust.'

Munkle's face ignited. 'You'll need a diversion. Me, Spitch and Lock will fly round the beastie wearing hover shoes, that way it'll be far too busy trying to munch us to notice you doin' magic…'

She turned to the elves. 'Now, Spitchy, Lock… prickle those pointies and baggle those bobbles. Let's save the boss man…'

THE NIGHT THEY NICKED SAINT NICK

Chapter 12

Santa's Little Helper

A minute later, Munkle, Spitch and Lock had checked their weapons, pulled on their hover-shoes and were ready to leave the cave.

Derek, his legs wobbling slightly, held the water bomb in one hand and a pinch of Elvun Dust in the other. Outside, he could hear the dragon pace angrily.

Derek felt a thick line of sweat on his brow. Sensing that three pairs of eyes were watching him closely, relying on him, he raised his hand over his head and let the dust spatter his silver hair. At once, he felt the tingling and the tickling, the shivering and the shuddering, as the magic started to work.

Munkle stepped forwards and hovered a foot above the ground. 'Right, Elves, let's Fudgebust a dragon...' In a flash, she zoomed through the cave entrance, followed by a determined looking Spitch and Lock.

Derek concentrated as hard as he could. Slowly, shakily, the water-bomb rose from his hand. It stopped a foot from his open palm as if on an invisible wire. Then he heard a terrific thunder of sound. Blasts and booms and shouts and roars.

Hesitantly, Derek took a step through the opening. His eyes widened as he saw the battle. The elves zipped round the dragon like flies, firing constantly, weaving up and down, ducking out of its way.

The dragon was furious; first it

lunged at Spitch, who dodged it with ease; then Munkle, who somersaulted through the air, missing its razor sharp teeth by a matter of inches. Then it rounded on Lock.

Mistiming his dive, Lock didn't see the dragon's tail until it was too late. It smashed into him, sending him crashing to the ground. He lay as still as a corpse.

Horrified, Derek wanted to run and see if Lock was alive, but there was no time. He had to stop the dragon. Concentrating on the floating bomb, he guided it closer to the dragon, waiting for its mouth to open.

Suddenly Munkle swung in front of the dragon, riding the air like a surfer on a wave. The dragon shot a firebolt at her. It missed. Then Munkle saw the water bomb. She faced the dragon head on and fired her Fudgebuster. No effect. The dragon pounced, its jaws wide open.

'NOW, DEREK!' Munkle cried, swerving away.

Derek sent the water bomb into the dragon's mouth like a basketball through a hoop.

'EXPLODE THE BOMB, DEREK!' Munkle shouted.

Derek gave a quick nod and concentrated hard.

Just then there was a muffled bang from inside the dragon's belly; wisps of silvery smoke streamed from its eyes. Then, astonishingly, the dragon began to inflate. Derek couldn't believe it. The dragon grew fatter and fatter as the stretchy water expanded in its tummy, its legs waving like crazy. It looked ridiculous, laughable even, like a giant green hot-air balloon.

Munkle glanced at Derek. 'Take cover… She's gonna blow!'

Derek dropped to the ground, his

head cradled in his arms.

BOOOOOM!! - the dragon exploded. Water shot everywhere, soaking Derek's scarlet robe.

A few moments later, all was still. His heart rushed as he saw the unguarded door to the dungeons. Quickly, he got to his feet. Then he remembered - Lock.

Looking over, he saw Munkle and Spitch kneeling beside their lifeless friend.

'Lock? Locky boy?' Spitch breathed, his eyes filling with tears.

Derek waddled over, his heart sinking further with each step.

'C'mon, Lieutenant Lock!' Munkle said desperately, her voice cracking. 'No one's dying on this mission...'

Suddenly Lock's eyelashes flickered and a weak grin curled on his mouth. 'I'm hungry,' he said in a very squeaky voice that seemed to be at odds with his squat, square, stocky body. After a few seconds of relieved hugs, Munkle and Spitch helped Lock to his feet.

Munkle turned to Derek, pride fixed on her face. 'You did it, kidder.'

'We did it…' Derek said.

Munkle smiled. 'So, do you want to meet Santa?'

Derek felt a rush of anticipation as they walked to the dungeons. He ran his hand across his chin. It felt very stubbly but certainly not a full beard. Santa had to be alive - the transformation wasn't complete.

Munkle banged twice on the door. 'Santa, it's Munkle. We're here to rescue you...'

There was no reply.

Munkle banged again. 'Santa, it's me … Elleana Munkle' There was fear in her voice now. 'It's a rescue!' She banged again. No reply. Was Santa conscious? Was he even in there?

Munkle looked very worried. 'Lock, blow the door. Santa, if you can hear me. Stand back.'

Lock fired the Bungle Cannon. KABOOM! The door exploded into tiny fragments. As the dust cloud settled, Derek could make out a figure lying in the corner, his large body twisted, his grey hair matted and dirty. The old man wore a long black robe. He looked weak and starved and broken.

Munkle ran at him and fell to her knees. 'Santa…Santa…It's Munkle!' Her eyes grew damp.

The old man didn't move.

Seconds passed. Then his eyelids slowly opened and his brilliant blue eyes stared back at Munkle.

'E - Elleana?' he slurred.

'Yes, sir,' Munkle choked. Tears streamed down her cheeks now. 'We're here to save you, sir. This is

Derek?' She ushered Derek to move forward.

'Hello, Mr Claus,' Derek said quietly.

The old man's eyes seemed to twinkle. A tinge of colour returned to his pale cheeks. 'H-hello, Derek.' Then his eyes rolled white and his body grew limp.

'Derek … the dust…' Munkle urged. 'Quick!'

Derek pulled off the pouch and poured the remaining dust over the old man's head. Then he waited.

Nothing happened - the old man's body lay as still as if carved from stone. Derek couldn't believe it … were they too late?

But then the old man's eyes snapped open, bursting with life. His head jerked up and a moment later, his hair and beard magically cleaned themselves and gleamed silver; his black robe, so dank and grimy, turned a breathtaking scarlet.

Santa Claus was back.

As Derek heard the elves squeal with joy, he realised something else. He felt different, lighter. His tummy had returned to its normal size. At once, he stroked his chin, it was silky smooth. He looked down and saw his dressing gown had turned deepest blue.

He was Derek Brundle again.

Chapter 13

A Pongy Punishment

Relief flooded Derek's body. He felt so happy. He wanted to shout and whistle and sing and dance. He watched awestruck as Santa Claus stood to his full height and looked down at them. He was as tall and thick and wide as a tree. His kindly eyes searched out Derek's and his face cracked into a melon-like smile that flickered as bright as any flame. 'That feels much better, Derek. I'm glad you got my message. I do hope I didn't ruin your sleep.'

'No, sir,' Derek breathed. 'You didn't.'

'I am glad,' Santa said.

Suddenly Munkle, Spitch and Lock launched themselves at Santa's waist, clinging like limpets to a rock, giving him the mightiest of hugs.

'Ho ho, my little friends … how lovely to see you again,' Santa beamed. 'Thank you so much for rescuing me, I do hope it didn't ruin your Christmas.'

Munkle looked up, her eyes red. 'There's no Christmas without you, boss.'

'How very kind of you, dear,' Santa said. 'But as we all know that's not true. There would have been a Christmas because of one very brave and very special young man.' His eyes settled on Derek, whose face flushed red. 'And I thank you, Derek. From the bottom of my heart, I thank you.' He gave a deep bow.

'Er, that's all right, Mr Claus,'

Derek said. 'We're all just really glad to have you back.'

'Thank you, Derek. But if I'm back, it's because of you.' He looked at the elves. 'Because of all of you. Now, what's the time? I believe I have some presents to deliver.'

Munkle hoisted her sleeve to reveal a reindeer shaped watch with antlers in place of the minute and hour hands. 'There's plenty o' time. We can get back to Poleland in time to do everythin'.'

'Of course we can,' Santa said, 'and we will. However, it would be wrong for a certain toymaker not to get his comeuppance, wouldn't it? Derek, shall you and I pay Charles Horridge a visit?'

Derek gave a reluctant nod. 'Er, okay.'

'Excellent. I do believe he's in the tallest tower, deciding whether or not to start crying like a baby.' Santa looked up at a red light on the dungeon ceiling and waved. 'Aren't you, Charles?'

A moment later, Spitch and Lock were jeering and pulling rude hand gestures at the camera.

Santa stretched out his arms. 'Please, everyone ... Stand back.'

Derek and the elves moved against the dungeon walls. They heard Santa click his fingers and - BOOM - a large pile dust and soil and rock crashed down from above. Light filled the room. Looking up, Derek saw a long, wide tunnel which led to the surface.

'Derek,' Santa said, holding out his hand. 'Take this.'

Derek did and suddenly he rose off the ground, floating through the dark, damp tunnel into daylight. They landed on a large patch of grass outside the castle walls. He watched as a breathless Munkle, Spitch and Lock landed beside them.

'Munkle,' Santa said. 'Can you make your own way back to Poleland?'

'Course, boss. You sure you don't want us to come with you?'

'No, thank you,' Santa said, grinning at Derek. 'Charles Horridge will rue the day he messed with two Father Christmases, eh?'

Moments later, Derek, his hand clinging tightly to Santa's, flew through the air to the tallest tower, the icy wind stabbing his face. Facing forward, he saw the lamp-lit room he'd seen earlier, when Santa clicked his fingers... BOOM ... an explosion blew out the window; chunks of stone and broken glass showered the ground, leaving a gaping hole in the tower wall. Santa guided them through and they touched down on soft carpet.

Derek saw they were standing in a dark, gloomy room with a long table in the centre and banks of television screens covering the walls; each screen showed a different room in the castle. At the table sat a scrawny, pale faced man with a dark pointed beard and cold grey eyes.

'Hello, Charles,' Santa said cheerily.

Charles Horridge looked petrified. 'P - Please, d - don't hurt me,' he cried, his trembling voice sounding very different from the mean and nasty one Derek had heard before.

'I'm Father Christmas,' Santa said. 'I think you've missed the point as to what I'm all about. I'm not going to hurt you.'

Horridge's body shivered with relief.

Santa's face grew serious and he gave a loud tut. 'However, much as I hate to do something like this, I really do think you should be punished. I mean, trying to deny the world a Christmas just so you can sell a few more badly made toys next year. That is a very sad state of affairs, isn't it?'

Santa strode calmly around the room. 'You see, Charles, what you fail to realise is that you can't deny the world a Christmas. No one can. And, as young Derek here proves, Christmas is about more than toys and presents and turkey dinners. It's about love and decency and respect and kindness. These are the real gifts of Christmas. And that's something you may never understand, I'm sad to say.'

Horridge's face turned tomato soup red. 'Pah!' Christmas is for fools and dreamers,' he growled. 'And fools deserve to be made fools of. Christmas is about money. Nothing more, nothing less…'

'And that is why you shall never

understand it,' Santa replied. 'You don't need money to enjoy Christmas. Look at you, you've always been rich and has it ever brought you even an ounce of happiness? I don't think so.'

Horridge shot Santa a very nasty look.

Santa smiled back. 'However, it's never too late to change. I'm going to make you do something good for everyone and, in time, it may please you in a way no amount of money ever could.'

'Whatever it is, I won't do it,' Horridge snapped.

Santa smiled. 'Oh, there's a wrapping troll named Dimplegog who begs to differ. You see, Dimplegog is chief wrapper at our largest wrapping station and I believe he needs an assistant. Unfortunately, he suffers from a terrible case of the trumples. And troll wind is the very worst kind.

No one wants to work with him. But I'm sure you'd be willing to do it, wouldn't you?'

Derek smothered a giggle.

Horridge looked horrified. 'I won't – I won't do it!'

Santa smiled. 'I think you will.' He clicked his fingers and, from nowhere, dozens of sheets of wrapping paper appeared ... hurtled towards a wide-eyed Horridge ... and bound his arms and feet tightly together.

'NOOOO!' Horridge screamed above the crunch and crackle of paper. He struggled and squirmed but it did no good. Within seconds, the only part of him free from paper was his head.

'Oh, yes...' Santa replied, clicking his fingers again.

Derek watched, astonished, as two things happened: first of all, a strawberry shoe-lace appeared and curled itself around Horridge's right ankle; then, a hundred small birds with dazzling red chests flew into the room and circled Horridge's head. Santa gave a sharp nod and the robins swooped down and scooped the strawberry shoe-lace in their beaks.

'Get off, you flying insects,' Horridge cried. 'GET OFF!'

Santa turned to the robins. 'My little friends, would you please take Mr Horridge to Poleland and inform High Commissioner Krinkle we have an assistant for Dimplegog.' Santa smiled at Horridge. 'I shall see you very soon, Charles. Good luck.'

Before Horridge had a chance to reply, he was yanked upside down and disappeared through the hole, screaming at the top of his lungs.

A very satisfied Santa turned to Derek. 'Shall we return to Poleland, young man? We really need to load up the sleigh if we're going to deliver all the presents together.'

Derek felt confused. 'Together?'

'Well ...' Santa grinned. 'Surely two Father Christmases are better than one?'

Chapter 14

The Departure Lounge

Several hours later, Derek stood surrounded by thousands of excited elves and trolls in a gigantic room called The Departure Lounge. Hundreds of fairies zipped joyfully through the air, leaving behind them a shimmering trail of silver fairy dust and a band of elves played Christmas songs on a range of very peculiar looking brass instruments, from a tiny trombone the length of a fishfinger to a trumpet the size of a small car.

Everyone faced a marble stage, set below a large clock that showed five minutes until midnight. On the stage stood a golden sleigh, crammed with presents and pulled by six magnificent reindeers, each looking thoroughly pleased with themselves and nodding self-importantly at the crowd.

At once, a hush rippled through the room as Santa Claus walked on stage and picked up an icicle-shaped microphone. 'Elves, trolls and fairies … in precisely five minutes it will be Christmas Day and our annual deliveries shall begin.'

The crowd roared with delight.

'Now, my friends, as you are all aware, this Christmas has been fraught with problems. Indeed, it is only because of the noble actions of a few brave elves that I'm here to talk to you on this, the most special of nights. Good citizens of Poleland, I give you Special Elf Service Agents Captain Elleana Munkle, Lieutenant Eggadore

Spitch, and Lieutenant Gubblins Lock...'

The Departure Lounge erupted with cheers and hoots and whistles.

Munkle, Spitch and Lock walked on stage to be met by Santa, who shook each of their hands and pinned a shiny medal to their jackets.

Santa extended his arms and again, the room fell silent.

'And, of course, I'd like to thank High Commissioner Allicia Krinkle, Ribbergob Buntleflip and Special Elf Service Agent, Rebbenta Greta, for their part in my rescue.'

Again, the crowd cheered as Krinkle, Buntleflip and Greta climbed the steps, shook Santa's hand, and joined Munkle, Spitch and Lock at the side of stage.

Santa waited for the applause to settle. 'And finally...' A proud smile crossed his face. 'What can I say about our special guest? He's been on my good boy list from the moment he was born, he's the pride of the man-folk world, and if he wishes, after my time has passed, will be the world's next Santa Claus. Ladies and gentle-elves, I give you the real saviour of Christmas … Derek Brundle.'

The crowd had saved their loudest cheers for last.

A humbled and very nervous Derek climbed the steps and shook Santa's hand. To his surprise, he felt Santa slip something into his palm. He recognised it at once: a pouch of Elvun Dust.

'Merry Christmas, Derek,' Santa said warmly. 'It would be a shame not to have some magic should you need it.'

Derek beamed with delight.

Santa pointed at the sleigh. 'Well, Derek, if you'd care to climb aboard, I think it's time to take you home, don't you?'

Derek nodded. Then he felt a small hand on his shoulder. He turned round to see Munkle, a can of wakey wakey spray in her tiny hand.

'Think your mum and dad might need this,' Munkle said, passing it over.

Derek grinned. 'I think they might.'

And then Munkle flung her arms round Derek and they hugged like very old friends. 'I'll miss you, kidder,' she said, tears leaking from her eyes.

'I'll miss you too, Munkle.'

Then a deafening chime echoed through the Departure Lounge. The clock struck twelve. Suddenly, the air was filled with bangs and crackles and fizzes as thousands of fireworks exploded high above them in a sea of colour.

'Come on, Derek,' Santa shouted

above the roar of the crowd. 'Let's go to work ...'

Derek nodded and climbed aboard the sleigh.

Santa settled himself onto the driver's seat, then fumbled in his pockets and pulled out a handful of Elvun Dust. He scattered some over the reindeer's heads, who snorted happily, their antlers glowing silver as the dust's magic began to take effect.

The firework display ended as the clock reached its last chime and the crowd hushed with anticipation.

At once, Santa shouted. 'DUMPTON, LUMPTON, FLUMPTON, KRUMPTON, SCRUMPTON and BLUMPTON…' The reindeers looked up, recognising their names. 'LET'S GIVE THE WORLD A CHRISTMAS TO REMEMBER…'

His broad smile grew into a laugh.

'HO HO HO… MERRY CHRISTMAS, POLELAND! YEEEEE HAAAAAAHHH!'

The crowd roared as the reindeers broke into a gallop. Derek watched as their thundering hooves left the stage and climbed the air, his tummy lurching wildly. Within moments, they were flying.

Looking up, Derek saw a hatch open in the ceiling. Taking the opportunity for one last, lingering look at Poleland, he faced forward and watched the twinkling night sky get ever closer.

As Santa steered the sleigh higher, Derek felt the first cooling flecks of snow upon his face. Within seconds, it fell thick and fast. He took a deep and very happy breath and let the wonder of the moment wash over him. It really had been the most remarkable Christmas Eve and was turning into the most magical Christmas Day.

Furthermore, he knew that one day he would become the next Santa Claus. And he couldn't think of anything better than that…

CARL ASHMORE

Carl is a children's writer from Crewe, England. He has written six books for children: 'The Time Hunters,' 'The Time Hunters and the Box of Eternity,' 'The Time Hunters and the Spear of Fate,' 'The Time Hunters and the Sword of Ages', 'The Night They Nicked Saint Nick,' and 'Bernard and the Bibble.'

He is currently working on the fifth and final book in the Time Hunters series, 'The Time Hunters and the Lost City.'

He can be contacted at carlashmore@mailcity.com

21464905R00085

Printed in Poland
by Amazon Fulfillment
Poland Sp. z o.o., Wrocław